Engineer Arielle and the Israel Independence Day Surprise

For Myah and Zoey–D.B.C.

To Lilly and Itamar–Y.K.O.

© 2017 by by Deborah Bodin Cohen
Illustrations copyright © 2017 Lerner Publishing Group, Inc.
© Hanan Isachar/SuperStock, pg. 32.

KAR-BEN PUBLISHING
A division of Lerner Publishing Group, Inc.
241 First Avenue North
Minneapolis, MN 55401 USA
1-800-4-Karben

Website address: www.karben.com

Main body text set in BernhardGothic Medium.
Typeface provided by The Font Company.

Library of Congress Cataloging-in-Publication Data

Names: Cohen, Deborah Bodin, 1968– author. 1 Orrelle, Yael Kimhi, illustrator.
Title: Engineer Arielle and the Israel Independence Day surprise : high, low, and on the go / by Deborah Bodin Cohen ; illustrated by Yael Kimhi Orrelle.
Description: Minneapolis : Kar-Ben Publishing, [2017] 1 Summary: "Engineer Arielle drives her train through Jerusalem on Israel Independence Day, greeting friends and waiting to celebrate with her brother Ezra, who is the lead pilot in the Israeli Air Force's special air show"—Provided by publisher.
Identifiers: LCCN 2016028302 1 ISBN 9781512420944 (lb : alk. paper) 1 ISBN 9781512420951 (pb : alk. paper)
Subjects: 1 CYAC: Independence Day (Israel)—Fiction. 1 Railroad trains—Fiction. 1 Air pilots—Fiction. 1 Jews—Israel—Fiction. 1 Israel—Fiction.
Classification: LCC PZ7.C6623 Emk 2017 1 DDC [E]—dc23

LC record available at https://lccn.loc.gov/2016028302

Manufactured in the United States of America
1-41261-23236-9/15/2016

Engineer Arielle and the Israel Independence Day Surprise

By Deborah Bodin Cohen

illustrations by Yael Kimhi Orrelle

KAR-BEN
PUBLISHING

Engineer Arielle sang in the shower.
She grinned while brushing her teeth.

She skipped to her closet to put on her train conductor's uniform. Then she grabbed a rolled-up poster and danced toward the apartment door.

Mid-pirouette, Arielle heard her brother Ezra laugh.
"You're certainly happy today!"
"Of course I am!" said Arielle. "It's Israel's birthday!
Yom Ha'Atzma'ut!"

"It's too bad that we both have to work today while everybody else has a holiday," said Ezra. "We won't even get to see each other."

"Not true," Arielle reminded him. "I'll see you, even if you don't see me. Everybody in Israel will see you today!"

"I suppose you're right," chuckled Ezra.

Arielle looked at her watch. "Oops, I've got to go."

Arielle jumped onto her scooter, tucking her poster behind her seat. She zoomed off, weaving through Jerusalem's traffic.

Beep, beep! She passed the old train station. Trains no longer stopped at the old station. Now, cafes filled the space.

Arielle thought of her great-great-grandfather, Engineer Ari, who drove the first train from Tel Aviv to Jerusalem into that very station over 100 years ago. Arielle was named after him. "Great-Great-Grandpa Ari," whispered Arielle. "I'm a train engineer, just like you!"

Arielle rode her scooter up a hill and down into a valley. She passed falafel stands, vegetable markets, and playgrounds.

Beep, beep, zoom, zoom!

At Jerusalem's new light rail train station, she waved to the guard and parked her scooter.

Before every shift, Arielle inspected her sleek, beautiful train. But today she had a special task. Carrying the poster, she carefully climbed a ladder and taped the poster to the roof of the train.

In her conductor's seat, Arielle sat in front of her controls—computer screens, knobs, and levers. Lickety split, she started the train and pulled out of the station, right on time.

The train hummed toward its first stop. The doors opened with a buzz. Passengers piled into the train. **"Yom Ha'Atzma'ut sameach!"** called Arielle cheerfully. **"Happy Independence Day!"**

The train hummed through Jerusalem, picking up passengers and dropping them off.

Ring, ring. *Buzz, buzz.* Doors opened. Doors closed. *Hum, hum.* The train stopped at the Old City. A computerized voice announced, "Damascus Gate."

Arielle saw her friend Sarah getting off the train. "**Yom Ha'Atzma'ut sameach**, Sarah! Where are you headed?"

"I'm going to the Kotel," said Sarah. "Every Independence Day, I go to the Western Wall to put a note into the Wall praying for peace in Israel. How will you celebrate today, Arielle?"

"I'm going to celebrate with my brother. We'll all celebrate with him!"

"What do you mean?" asked Sarah.

But before Arielle could answer, Sarah was swept up in the crowd leaving the train, and waving good-bye.

Buzz, buzz. The doors closed. *Hum, hum.*
Arielle drove the train up Jaffa Road, where hundreds of
people had gathered for a street party. The computerized
voice announced, "Merkaz Yaffo, Jaffa Center."

Arielle spotted her cousin Talia, stepping off the train.

"It's so crowded here, I almost didn't see you," laughed Arielle. "Are you meeting somebody?"

"Yes! My friends from the army. Do you want to join us? You aren't going to work all day, are you?"

"I'll see Ezra later and celebrate with him," said Arielle. "We'll all celebrate with him!"

"What? Well, come meet us here. Text me when you finish work," said Talia. "Bring Ezra!"

"I don't think he can come," laughed Arielle.

Buzz, buzz. The doors closed. *Hum, hum.* The train started up a small hill. Arielle stopped the train at a large market. The computerized voice announced, "Machane Yehuda." Arielle saw her neighbor Eitan.

"Ah, Arielle," said Eitan. "I thought my wife had bought food for our Yom Ha'Atzma'ut barbecue. But *she* thought that *I* bought it. So, here I am at the *shuk,* the market. Are you going to a picnic or barbecue after work to celebrate the holiday?"

"I'll see my brother Ezra later," said Arielle. "And I'll celebrate with him. We'll all celebrate with him!"

"All Israel celebrates together, doesn't it?" said Eitan. "One *mishpachah,* one family."

Buzz, buzz. The doors closed. *Hum, hum.* The train continued on. Arielle pulled into the train stop at the central bus station. From there, travelers could go anywhere in Israel.

Arielle saw two of her friends getting off the train with backpacks.

"Jesse! Benny! Where are you headed?"

"Tel Aviv," said Benny.

"I'm going to visit Independence Hall, where David Ben-Gurion declared Israel a country in 1948," said Jesse.

"I just want to go to the beach," laughed Benny. "Come with us, Arielle."

"I can't," laughed Arielle. "I have a train to drive. Besides, I'll see my brother later and celebrate with him. We'll all celebrate with him!"

"Bring your brother to Tel Aviv!" called Benny.

"He's already going to Tel Aviv," laughed Arielle. "And to Haifa, Tiberias, Beersheva, and Eilat."

Buzz, buzz. The doors closed. *Hum, hum.* The train continued on, over a magnificent bridge built to look like King David's harp.

Arielle heard rumbling in the air. The moment had arrived.

A group of Israeli Air Force planes roared across the horizon. The planes twirled, pranced and pirouetted against the blue sky, leaving a white trail that spelled "Israel."

Arielle stopped the train and spoke into the microphone. "**Yom Ha'Atzma'ut sameach**, my friends. My brother Ezra is flying the lead plane. I taped a sign to the train's roof for him to see. Let's go outside and celebrate with him!"

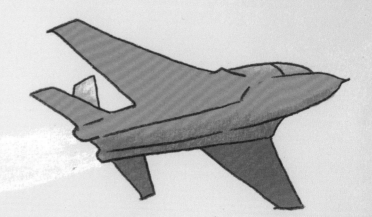

People eagerly scrambled off the train and onto the bridge.

Arielle held her breath as Ezra's plane roared through the sky.

Then Ezra dipped low toward the train bridge.
He waved from the cockpit.

Arielle and the passengers cheered.
"Yom Ha'Atzma'ut sameach!"

Happy Independence Day, Israel!

Author's Note

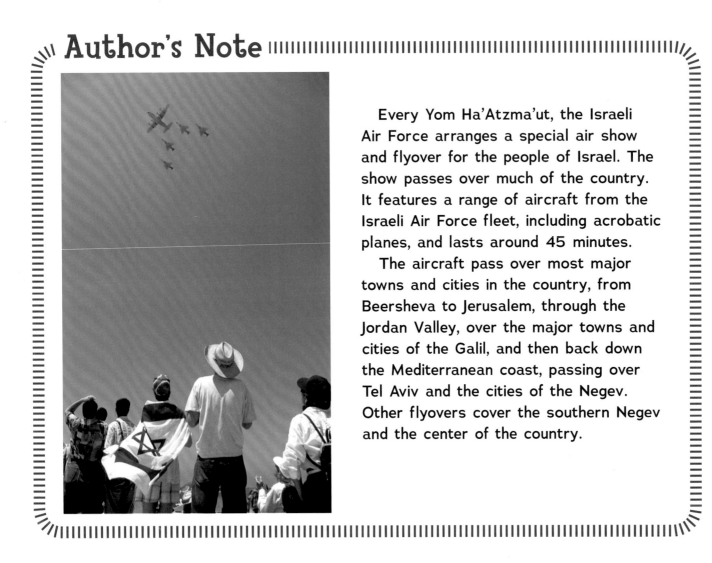

Every Yom Ha'Atzma'ut, the Israeli Air Force arranges a special air show and flyover for the people of Israel. The show passes over much of the country. It features a range of aircraft from the Israeli Air Force fleet, including acrobatic planes, and lasts around 45 minutes.

The aircraft pass over most major towns and cities in the country, from Beersheva to Jerusalem, through the Jordan Valley, over the major towns and cities of the Galil, and then back down the Mediterranean coast, passing over Tel Aviv and the cities of the Negev. Other flyovers cover the southern Negev and the center of the country.